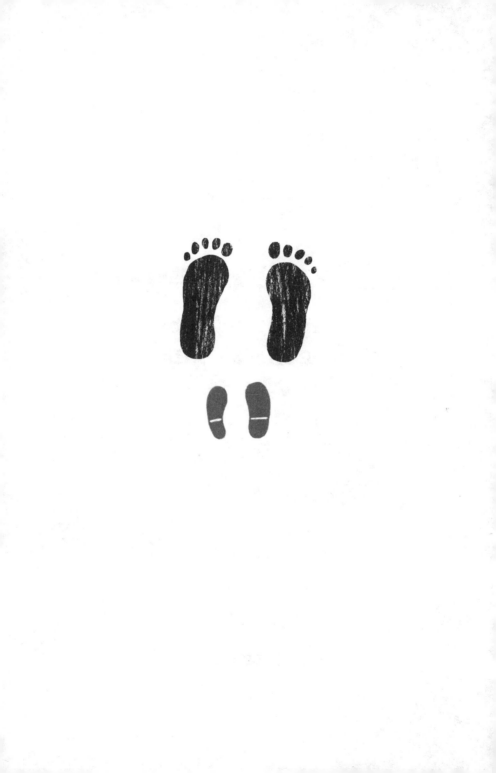

By **Ellen Potter**

Illustrated by
**Felicita Sala**

**AMULET BOOKS**

NEW YORK

# BIG FOOT
## and LITTLE FOOT

Cataloging-in-Publication Data has been applied for and may be obtained from the Library of Congress.
ISBN 978-1-4197-2859-4

Text copyright © 2018 Ellen Potter
Illustrations copyright © 2018 Felicita Sala
Book design by Siobhán Gallagher

Printed and bound in U.S.A.
10 9 8 7 6 5 4 3

Amulet Books are available at special discounts when purchased in quantity for premiums and promotions as well as fundraising or educational use. Special editions can also be created to specification. For details, contact specialsales@abramsbooks.com or the address below.

**ABRAMS** The Art of Books
195 Broadway, New York, NY 10007
abramsbooks.com

For Addison, Natalie, Ethan, and Violet
Waterman, who are always ready for an
adventure in the Big Wide World.

# 1

## Hugo

Deep in the cold North Woods, there lived a young Sasquatch named Hugo. He was bigger than you but smaller than me, and he was hairier than both of us. He lived in apartment 1G in the very back of Widdershins Cavern with his mother and father and his older sister, Winnie.

Even though the apartment was very small, there was a nice little stream that ran right into Hugo's bedroom. It entered through a hole in the bottom of the stone wall, traveled across the room, and then escaped out another hole in the wall by Hugo's toy chest.

Hugo had carved a little wooden boat that was small enough to sail in the stream.

He pretended that he was the captain of the boat and he was sailing to Bora Bora or Atlantic City or some other mysterious place that his grandfather had told him about. He'd make storms by swirling his hand in the stream, and the toy boat would wobble wildly but wouldn't topple.

Sometimes little fish swam into his bedroom. They were on their way to Ripple Worm River, which ran through the North Woods. Hugo pretended the fish were sharks and that they were attacking his boat. He made the noise of a shark *splooshing* out of the ocean and clacking its teeth. (Sasquatches are excellent at making pretend noises. For instance, if you are in the woods and hear a howl, you may, in fact, be hearing a Sasquatch pretending to be a coyote.)

The fish played with Hugo for a while, but in the end they always swam out through the hole in the wall and into the Big Wide World, where Hugo was never allowed to go.

## 2

## Hair Balls

Each morning, Hugo and his sister, Winnie, walked to school. Because their apartment was at the east end of the cavern, and their school was at the west end, Hugo and Winnie had to walk quite a long way. The cavern floor was icy cold against their bare feet, and their breath made cloudy puffs as they walked along.

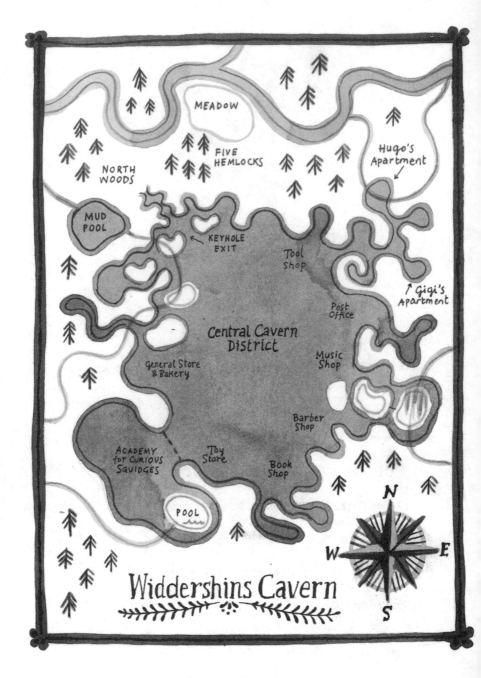

Widdershins Cavern

"Do you think sharks would eat a Sasquatch?" Hugo asked Winnie.

"Don't be a pinhead, Hugo," said Winnie. She was always grumpy in the morning. "There aren't any sharks in a cavern."

"But I might become a sailor. And if I ran into a shark, I'd like to know if it would eat me."

"Sasquatches *don't* become sailors," Winnie told him.

"Maybe sometimes they do," Hugo said.

"No, never," said Winnie firmly.

Winnie then stopped in front of apartment 1B. She gave a quick rap on the door. The door opened, and her friend Hazel came out.

Winnie and Hazel rubbed their elbows

together and bumped their hips together and then said, "Hakkah-makka-momo."

That's because they were in a secret club, except it wasn't very secret since everyone at school knew about it. Anyway, the only thing they ever did in the club was make their own lip gloss.

Right behind Hazel came Hazel's younger sister, Gigi. She was a small

Sasquatch, as Sasquatches go. She had three thin braids down the right side of her head and very good posture.

As they walked along, Hugo asked, "Gigi, do you think a Sasquatch could become a sailor?"

Gigi thought for a minute. She was a slow but excellent thinker.

"It's possible," she said.

Hugo's spirits lifted.

"But," Gigi added, "the Sasquatch would have to be VERY careful not to be seen by Humans."

"Of course." Hugo nodded seriously. A Sasquatch could never

be seen by Humans. That was the Most Important Rule.

"He'd need a boat, too," said Gigi.

*That was no problem,* thought Hugo.

Sasquatches were good builders. They could build just about anything from logs.

"And he would have to bring along five barrels of blackberries and twenty jars of acorn butter for the trip," Gigi added.

"Right!" said Hugo. He'd bring thirty jars of acorn butter, since that was his favorite thing to eat.

"And do you think a shark would eat a Sasquatch?" Hugo asked.

Gigi snorted. "Of course not! Eating a Sasquatch would give a shark hair balls."

"Phew, that's a relief," said Hugo.

Gigi thought some more.

"There's something else a Sasquatch would need," she said. "A Navigator."

"A Navigator." Hugo nodded thoughtfully. After a moment he asked, "Is that anything like an alligator?"

"No, Hugo. A Navigator is someone who knows all about the Big Wide World. A Navigator tells you which way to go."

"Oh." *That might be a problem*, thought Hugo. Sasquatches don't know about the Big Wide World. They only know about caves and trees and acorn butter and berries and the deep, cold woods.

### 3

## The Academy for Curious Squidges

ven though Hugo's school was in a cave, it was a cozy, cheerful-looking place. Painted in loopy yellow letters above the door were the words THE ACADEMY FOR CURIOUS SQUIDGES. (A "squidge," in case you don't know, is what you call a young Sasquatch.) There were three classrooms in the Academy. Classroom One

was for the youngest squidges. Classroom Two was for squidges who were old
enough to know better. Classroom Three
was for squidges who *thought* they knew
better than everyone else but really didn't.

Hugo was in Classroom One. Behind
the teacher's desk, colorful letters of the

alphabet hung across the wall on a long string. In a corner of the classroom, by a reading loft that looked like a tree house, there were posters of plants and flowers and berries. The posters either said Yum! or Blech! This was to help squidges figure out what was safe to eat in the woods.

Hugo and Gigi went to their cubbies to put away their backpacks. Their classmate Izzy was there, too.

"Hi, Izzy," Hugo said.

"Hi, Yooho," Izzy replied. "I got a new packa monsta cobs." Izzy wore headgear for his overbite, so it was sometimes hard to understand him.

"What did he say?" Gigi whispered to Hugo.

"He says he got a new pack of Monster Cards," Hugo translated.

Izzy reached into his backpack and pulled out a small blue-and-yellow rectangular package. On it were the words MAD MARVIN'S MONSTER CARDS. COLLECT THEM ALL!

"Any good ones?" Hugo asked.

Izzy handed the package to Hugo. There were three cards in the package plus a flat piece of boysenberry gum. One of the Monster Cards had a picture of a

Fish-Tailed Goat, which looks exactly the way you think it would. Another card was of a Lumpen Murch, which is a bumpy black creature that lives in volcanoes and drinks hot lava. The last one was a Snoot-Nosed Gint, a giant lizard with a spike on its head. The picture on the card showed the Snoot-Nosed Gint perched on a tree limb, its mouth wide open to show its sharp teeth.

"Hey," said Hugo, "I'll trade you some Stink Sap for the Snoot-Nosed Gint." He reached into his backpack and pulled out a yellowy-green ball. This was Stink Sap. If you rolled it around in your hand, it got warm and squishy and smelled very bad. That was all it did, really, but each

Stink Sap smelled different, so that was interesting.

Izzy took the Stink Sap and rolled it around in his hand. Then he gave it a sniff.

*"Ewww!"* he said. He thought for a moment. "Okay." He put the Stink Sap in his backpack and handed the Snoot-Nosed Gint card to Hugo.

Hugo read the back of the card: "The Snoot-Nosed Gint spends most of its time in trees. Although its long, sharp teeth look fearsome, its most deadly weapon is the spike on its head, which is poisonous."

Hugo turned the card over to look at the picture again. "I'm glad Snoot-Nosed Gints aren't real."

"Actually," Gigi said, "someone once

claimed to see a Snoot-Nosed Gint right outside their cave."

Hugo shuddered. Sometimes he wished Gigi didn't know absolutely everything.

All the squidges rushed to their seats when their teacher, Mrs. Nukluk, walked into the classroom. She was wearing her long white cloak made of goose feathers. She wore that cloak every day, even in the summer. She said it was because she grew up in a cave way down south where it was all sunshiny, and she had never gotten used to the cold North Woods.

"Good morning, class! One, two, three, eyes on me," said Mrs. Nukluk. "We have lots to do today, so everyone take out your homework."

Everyone took out their homework and put it on their desks. Everyone except Malcolm. As usual, Malcolm had some of his breakfast stuck to his chest fur. Today, it was granola.

"Where's your homework, Malcolm?" asked Mrs. Nukluk.

"It's still in my pencil," he answered.

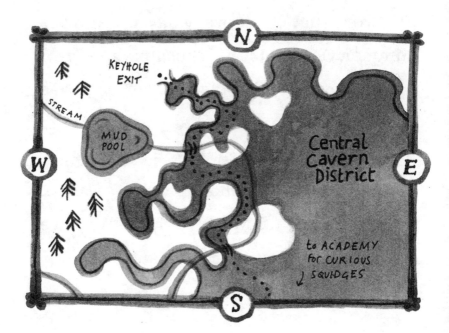

Mrs. Nukluk sighed.

The class worked on math first, then spelling, and after spelling came everyone's favorite subject—Hide and Go Sneak. All the students lined up by the door, hopping with excitement. They followed Mrs. Nukluk down a long, narrow passage under spiky stalactites, which looked just like icicles dripping from the cave's ceiling.

They turned this way and that through

a maze of tunnels. It was easy for a squidge to get lost, because there were many different tunnels that led nowhere at all, and some that led straight back to where you had just come from. But Mrs. Nukluk knew the way perfectly, and finally they came to the cavern entrance. The entrance was shaped like a keyhole, so they all had to turn sideways to get through it. Malcolm and Pip got stuck because they were both trying to get through at the same time, but Mrs. Nukluk sorted them out.

Now they were all outside, in the North Woods.

## 4

## Hide and Go Sneak

Being in the woods was serious business. Everyone had to be very, very quiet in case there were Humans around. First Mrs. Nukluk sniffed the air. Then she took a few sneaky steps to have a look around. Her footsteps made no noise at all. She made a small *"Hoot-hoot!"* which meant, "The coast is clear!"

It was so exciting to be outside, under the big sky! Hugo loved feeling the cold, fresh air on his face. It was the same air that had traveled over mountains and oceans, from all the far-

away places his grandfather had told him about. Just the thought of that gave Hugo a thrill.

The first thing all the squidges did was
to jump into the chilly mud pool beside the
cave. They smeared themselves with the
cold, thick mud from head to toe. After that
they rolled around on the forest floor, let-
ting leaves and twigs stick onto their muddy
bodies. Soon their long reddish fur was the
same brown-gray of a rock or a tree trunk,
with bits of leaves and twigs clinging to it.

Mrs. Nukluk inspected all her students.

"Well done," she proclaimed. "Now,
let's see you Sneak. Just over to the five

hemlock trees, around the burdocks, and back. One at a time, please."

One by one, the squidges took their turn at a Sneak. First was Gigi. You couldn't hear her steps at all. But she was always best at everything in school.

Next was Malcolm.

"Your feet are thumping again, Malcolm," warned Mrs. Nukluk.

"Sorry, Mrs. Nukluk!!" he called back.

"Now you're *shouting,* Malcolm," Mrs. Nukluk said sternly. Then to herself she murmured, "Give me strength." She said that a lot when she spoke to Malcolm.

After Malcolm came Izzy. His headgear got caught in a tree branch, which snapped back noisily. But that wasn't really his fault.

Then it was Hugo's turn to Sneak. He put his left heel down first and then rolled on the edge of his foot till he got to his toes. Then he put down his right heel. Not a single twig snapped. Not a single bush rustled.

When he got to the first hemlock tree, he glanced at Mrs. Nukluk. He was certain that she would be smiling because he'd done such a good job.

But she wasn't smiling.

She wasn't even looking at him. She was sniffing the air. Suddenly she made a sound that went, *"Knoooodle-knoooodle koooo!"* It sounded like a bird. But Hugo knew what it really was.

It was a code for "Emergency! Human is coming!"

# 5

## The Human

Hugo dropped to the ground. He didn't move a muscle. That was what Mrs. Nukluk had taught all her students to do in an emergency like this one.

All the other squidges had dropped to the ground, too. They kept perfectly still, as only a Sasquatch can. If you didn't

know any better, you would have thought the squidges were mounds of muck and leaves.

Hugo listened hard for the sound of a Human approaching. At first, all he could hear was the gurgle and *splish* of Ripple Worm River, which was at the end of a meadow, just past the five hemlock trees.

Suddenly, though, he heard footsteps. They were not noisy footsteps, but they weren't quiet either. Closer and closer they came. Hugo knew he was supposed

to squeeze his eyes shut, but he also did not want to miss his first glimpse of a real Human. His heart was pounding in his chest, and his stomach felt queasy with excitement and fear.

Suddenly, there was a rustle to the left of him. From behind the closest hemlock tree it appeared . . . a real, live *Human*!

The Human walked slowly, looking around as if it expected to see something interesting. Hugo was surprised at how small it was. Not much bigger than a Sasquatch toddler. And though Hugo expected to be terrified at the sight of the Human, he found he wasn't scared at all.

Hugo watched as the Human bent down and plucked up a dandelion puff. The Human closed its eyes for a moment, puckered up its lips, and blew. The dandelion puff broke apart and floated off in the wind.

It was such a strange thing to do, and

the Human looked so funny—with no hair on its body, except for a messy tuft on top of its head—that Hugo laughed.

The Human looked right at him.

Hugo's eyes went wide. So did the Human's. For a moment they were both frozen, staring at each other.

The very next moment rocks began to

fly at the Human. Hugo knew it was Mrs. Nukluk throwing the rocks, but she was so well hidden that it looked like the rocks were flying out of thin air. The rocks came close to the Human without actually hitting it, but that was enough to scare it. The Human turned and ran without looking back.

# 6

## Dead Porcupines

Once they were all safely back in the cavern, Mrs. Nukluk turned to Hugo. She was furious.

"In all my years of teaching," said Mrs. Nukluk, "not one of my students has ever been spotted by a Human . . . until today. And certainly none of them has *laughed* at the sight of one!" She was so mad that even the feathers on her long cloak were all puffed up, just like those of an angry goose. "What were you thinking, Hugo?"

"I was thinking . . ." said Hugo in a small-ish voice, "I was thinking that the Human was funny looking."

"There is *nothing* funny about Humans!" Mrs. Nukluk snapped. "You might have been captured. Or worse. I'll be sending a note home to your parents, Hugo, you can be sure of that!" Mrs. Nukluk took a deep breath and smoothed down the feathers on her cloak. "Now, everyone . . . go wash that mud off."

The class headed over to the underground pool just beside the classroom. All the squidges were splashing and playing

in the cold spring water. They were all having fun, except for Hugo. He was crushed. He'd never had a note sent home to his parents before.

"What did the Human look like up close?" Pip asked Hugo excitedly, as she

rubbed mud from the hair on her arms. "Did it have glowing red eyes?"

"That's just a myth," Gigi said.

"Its eyes were brown," said Hugo, "like ours."

"And did it smell like dead porcupines?" asked Malcolm. "I heard Humans stink."

Hugo shook his head. "No, it smelled . . ." Hugo tried to remember the Human's smell but couldn't. Hugo dunked his head underwater and scrubbed the mud out of his ears. When he popped his head back up, he remembered something.

"Gigi," he said, "I saw the Human do something strange. It plucked a dandelion puff, closed its eyes, and blew on it so that all the little seeds blew away. Why would it do that?"

"Oh, that's easy," said Gigi. "It was making a wish. I read about that once in a book. Humans blow on the dandelion so that the wish blows off into the Big Wide World and can come true."

"Oh." Hugo nodded. After a minute he asked, "Does it work?"

"It must," Gigi said thoughtfully, "or else why would they keep doing it?"

# 7

## Big Trouble

After school, Hugo and Winnie went to the Central Cavern District, where their mother and father and grandfather ran the Everything-You-Need General Store and Bakery. There were lots of other stores in the Central Cavern District. There was a barbershop and a toy store, where you

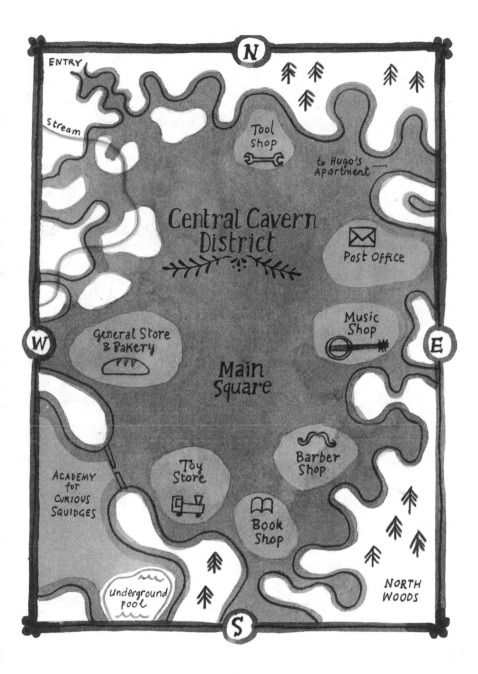

could get things like Stink Sap. There was a bookshop and there was a post office that took your letters to caves that were as far as five hundred miles away.

The little bell on the Everything-You-Need General Store and Bakery door rang when Hugo and Winnie stepped inside. Their grandfather was behind the cash register, ringing up Mrs. Rattlebags's order while she complained about the price of hazelnut flour.

"Your snacks are on the table," Grandpa called to Hugo and Winnie.

Hugo and Winnie sat down at the round

café table. On it, there was a stack of acorn butter-and-raspberry cream sandwiches, a bowl of walnuts with the shells still on (Hugo and Winnie like to crack the shells with their teeth), and two glasses of pale-green wild-mint juice. As delicious as it all looked, Hugo had no appetite. He was too worried about Mrs. Nukluk's note.

"How was school?" Mom asked, as she

and Dad walked out of the kitchen, their hands stained pink with gooseberries.

"Hugo got in trouble today," said Winnie right away. Even though Winnie wasn't in Hugo's class, word of bad behavior always spread quickly around their school.

Hugo kicked her under the table, and Winnie screeched.

"Enough," Mom said to them both sternly.

"What happened, Hugo?" Dad asked.

Hugo dug into his backpack and pulled out the note. A note from a teacher is never a happy thing, especially when the note says that your very own squidge was

**44**

not only spotted by a Human, but was spotted because he *laughed* at it.

"Laughing at a human, Hugo?? A HUMAN?!" Mom cried after she read the note.

"Humans are no laughing matter," Dad said. "They're dangerous creatures."

"Sometimes I wish I *were* a Human," mumbled Hugo.

"What did you say?" his dad asked.

"He said he wishes he were a Human," Winnie repeated loudly.

"Nonsense," said his mom.

"But I *do* wish I were a Human!" Hugo shouted. "Then I could walk around in the Big Wide World without always Sneaking. I could sail ships and see alligators and sharks and maybe even Snoot-Nosed

Gints, instead of being stuck in a cave my whole entire life!"

Mrs. Rattlebags gasped at this. "The squidge has lost his mind," she declared. "To wish he were a Human, of all things!"

"Hmmph," grunted Grandpa. "I suppose that Humans are no worse than Sasquatches. Some are good and some are bad and some are just a pain in the tush." He gave Mrs. Rattlebags a look.

After Hugo's outburst, his parents sent him straight home to his room, to think about what he'd done. Miserable, he sat on the floor by the stream and watched as tiny silverfish swam into the bedroom. He dipped his hand in the water, and the fish swam between his fingers, playing.

"I wish you were sharks," he said to the

fish. They tickled his fingers. "I wish I had a boat and a Navigator and that I could have adventures of my own." Then he thought of something. If the little Human could make a wish on a dandelion puff, why couldn't *he* make a wish, too? Except he didn't have a dandelion puff. And how could your wish be carried off into the Big Wide World without a dandelion puff to blow on?

He frowned and swished his fingers in the water, making a mini whirlpool, thinking. Suddenly he had an idea. He *did* have something he could send out into the Big Wide World!

He opened his toy chest and took out his little carved boat. He held it in his hand and closed his eyes, exactly like the Human had done.

Then he made a wish.

"I wish I could have an adventure," he said. Gently, he placed his boat in the stream and blew on it, just like the Human had blown on the dandelion. He blew and blew until the little boat sailed through the hole in the bottom of his wall and out into the Big Wide World.

# 8

## More Bad News

Nothing happened. Not a single thing. His wish did not come true.

Plus, the next day, there was more bad news at school. Mrs. Nukluk announced that because Hugo had been spotted by a Human, there would be no more Hide and Go Sneak classes for the rest of the semester.

"No fair!" all the squidges cried.

"Yeah! How come we all have to be punished for the dumb thing that Hugo did?" said Malcolm.

Hugo slumped down in his seat. He'd never felt so terrible in his life.

At recess, no one would play with him. If there was a game of Five Rocks, Two Sticks and Hugo asked to play, the other

squidges would say, "Sorry, the game just ended." And they'd walk away to do something else. Even Izzy was mad at him. Hugo had brought in an extra-rare Monster Card to show him, but Izzy just shrugged and walked away.

"Don't worry, Hugo," Gigi said as she patted his back. "By next week the class will forget they're mad at you."

He wanted to believe her, he really did. But after all, Gigi was the one who'd told him about wishes coming true if you blew on a dandelion puff. And so far, the only thing that had changed was that everyone was angry with him.

But then, three days later, something finally *did* happen.

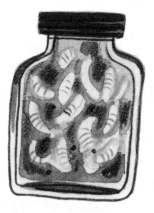

# 9

## *Rick-a-tick-tick*

Hugo was lying in bed, almost asleep, when he heard it. *Rick-a-tick-tick.*

At first Hugo thought it was a mouse. Sometimes mice would creep into his room, looking for a warm place to sleep at night. That was okay with Hugo. He didn't mind mice at all.

He closed his eyes and started to drift back to sleep.

*Rick-a-tick-tick.*

Hugo opened his eyes again. *That doesn't sound like mice*, he thought. He sat up and reached under his bed, pulling out his jar of glowworms. He jiggled the jar until the worms began to twist and turn. Gradually the worms started to glow brighter and brighter, until they gave off a greenish light. Holding the jar up to light his way, Hugo hopped out of bed to investigate.

*Rick-a-tick-tick.*

Quickly, Hugo turned his jar toward the noise. What he saw made him gasp in surprise. Floating on the stream in his room was his little toy boat. It had returned to him. Except now, there was something *rick-a-tick-ticking* inside it as the boat wobbled in the water.

Carefully, Hugo picked up the boat. Inside it was a little plastic toy in the shape of a Human. Its tiny feet were attached to a

funny little board with wheels on the bottom. The wheels even spun.

*Who does this belong to?* thought Hugo. *Not a Sasquatch. Sasquatches don't have toys like this. It must belong to a Human.*

Hugo held the toy in his hand, looking down at it in wonder. Something that came from the Big Wide World was sitting in the palm of his hand! Maybe his wish was beginning to come true. It wasn't an adventure, exactly . . . but it did seem like the start of one.

## 10

## Secret Project

There was no school the next day. That was a good thing, because Hugo was busy.

All morning long he worked on his secret project. He only came out of his room for hazelnut pancakes for breakfast, which he gobbled down before hurrying back to work.

"What are you doing in here?" Winnie flung open his bedroom door and squinted at him suspiciously.

"Stuff," Hugo said.

"Stuff? What kind of stuff?" Winnie asked, planting her hands on her hips.

"Hey, Winnie, guess what I found," Hugo said.

"What?" she asked, perking up with interest.

"Your nose," Hugo said. "It was in my business again."

"Ha ha," Winnie said and slammed the door.

Finally, just before lunch, Hugo finished. He held up his creation and inspected it.

"You're perfect," he whispered to it. It was a tiny Sasquatch. Hugo had carved it out of white pine. It was almost exactly the size of the Human toy but much more detailed. You could see the little fingers and toes. You could even see tiny fingernails and toenails. There were little smidgy lines carved into it for the hair, and its face looked a little like Hugo's.

Carefully, Hugo placed it in his boat. Since he had kept the Human toy, it was only fair to give the Human a Sasquatch toy. It was kind of like trading Monster Cards.

With four or five huffy breaths, Hugo sent the boat sailing out into the Big Wide World once again.

## 11

## Bigfoot

The boat came sailing back into his room the very next day. The carved Sasquatch was gone. In its place was a little jar with a folded piece of paper inside it.

A note! A note from someone in the Big Wide World! Hugo unscrewed the jar's lid. He tipped the jar upside down and shook out the note, then unfolded it. This was what it said:

MY NAME IS BOONE. I'M ALMOST TEN YEARS OLD. I'M SMALL FOR MY AGE BUT MY GRANDMA SAYS I'M FASTER THAN A SNEEZE THROUGH A SCREEN DOOR. DO YOU BELIEVE IN BIGFOOT?

BOONE

Hugo reread the note a few times. The last question puzzled him. What was Bigfoot? It sounded like one of the monsters in Mad Marvin's Monster Cards, but he'd never seen a Bigfoot card.

*How can I answer the note if I don't know what Bigfoot is?* he thought.

Then he had an idea. He jumped up and ran out of his apartment. He ran down the

long, winding cave hall to apartment 1B
and knocked on the door.

The door opened. Gigi was standing
there, holding a very fat book called *Everything You've Ever Wanted to Know About
Obtuse Triangles,* with one finger stuck in
the middle to mark her page.

"Hello, Hugo," said Gigi.

"What's a Bigfoot?" Hugo asked her.

"I'm looking at it," she said, gazing back
at him.

Hugo lowered his voice. "You mean . . . there's one . . . is there one *here*?" He looked behind him nervously.

"*You're* a Bigfoot, Hugo," said Gigi.

"My feet aren't big. They're just regular."

"I'm a Bigfoot, too," Gigi explained. "We all are. 'Bigfoot' is what Humans call Sasquatches."

Hugo considered that. "It's not very nice," said Hugo.

Gigi shrugged. "Any other questions?"

Hugo shook his head.

"Okay. See you later, Hugo," she said and shut the door.

Back in his room, Hugo wrote his reply:

MY NAME IS HUGO

AND I DO BELIEVE IN BIGFOOT. I LIVE IN
THE NORTH WOODS. WHERE DO YOU LIVE?
HAVE YOU EVER BEEN TO BORA BORA OR
ATLANTIC CITY?

   HUGO

He sent the boat out through the hole
in his wall and smiled. Knowing someone
who lived in the Big Wide World made him
feel like he was part of the Big Wide World,
too—part of the hills and the fields and Ripple Worm River and Bora Bora and everything in between.

## 12

## Acts of Bavewy

At school, Mrs. Nukluk had a big announcement.

"As you all know, the Frog Moon Festival will be this Saturday," she said. "Each year, we hold the festival to scare away winter so that spring will come to the North Woods." Mrs. Nukluk wrapped her feather cloak tighter around her body. "Finally."

Hugo loved the Frog Moon Festival. It was always lots of fun. The squidges wore scary masks, and there were races and games and loads of good food, like walnut pie and mushroom casserole and acorn-butter cookies and gooseberry pie.

"As usual, one class will perform a special ceremony at the Frog Moon Festival. Who knows what that is?" Mrs. Nukluk asked.

Izzy's hand shot up. "Acts of Bavewy," he said.

"Very good, Izzy. And why do we perform Acts of Bravery?"

Gigi raised her hand, and Mrs. Nukluk called on her.

"It's a rite of passage. It shows that

we are brave enough to become big Sas-quatches and have more responsibility."

"Very good, Gigi." Mrs. Nukluk looked around at all the squidges with an excited gleam in her eyes. "Well, class, at this year's Frog Moon Festival, *our class* will be performing the Acts of Bravery!"

Some Squidges cheered, but others looked nervous. The squidges who per-formed Acts of Bravery had to do some-thing they were afraid to do.

Malcolm raised his hand. "I'll fight a bear," he said.

"Think again," said Mrs. Nukluk.

"Okay, I'll shove a stick up my nose," Malcolm said.

"You did that the other day. It didn't end well for you, did it, Malcolm?" said Mrs.

Nukluk with raised eyebrows. Then she glanced around at the rest of the class and said, "For the next few days, you can all think about what you would like to do for your Act of Bravery. In the meantime, we will start making our scary masks."

Mrs. Nukluk went to the art closet and took out long strips of bark, pots of glue made from pine tree resin, paints made of red and yellow river clay, paintbrushes, and other bits and bobs collected from the woods.

"Remember, everyone," she said as she handed out the supplies, "your masks must be *very* scary!"

The class got

right to work. Hugo started to make a mask that looked like a shark, with a long, pointy snout and a wide-open mouth full of shark teeth.

"What's your Act of Bravery going to be?" Hugo asked Gigi. Her mask looked like a crazy bird, with a short, fat beak and black crow feathers glued all over.

"I might let my Uncle Clive's pet rat sit on my head," said Gigi. "He's disgusting. The rat, I mean, not Uncle Clive. What about you?"

Hugo shrugged. "I'm not sure yet." As he worked, he tried to keep his mind on an Act of Bravery, but his thoughts kept drifting back to Boone.

"Hey, Gigi," Hugo said after a few minutes, "do you think a Sasquatch could be friends with a Human?"

"No," Gigi said right away, as she painted the beak on her mask.

"But you didn't even think about it," Hugo protested.

"I don't have to. It's impossible. Humans either want to kill Sasquatches or capture them."

Hugo didn't think Boone wanted to kill or capture him. "My grandfather thinks Humans are probably just like Sasquatches. Some are good, and some are bad," Hugo said.

Gigi put down her paintbrush and looked at him. "When have you ever heard of a *good* Human, Hugo?"

## 13

## 100% True

ugo sat in his room, trying to do his homework, but he just kept thinking about what Gigi had said. Could it be true that all Humans were bad? Gigi *did* always seem to know everything. And in all the stories Hugo had ever heard about Humans, they were doing bad things to Sasquatches.

Still, he couldn't believe that Boone was *that* kind of Human.

Just then he heard a *clink-a-tink-tink* sound. He looked down at the little stream in his room. Sailing through the hole in the wall was his little boat, with the jar clinking inside it. Eagerly, Hugo picked up the jar, opened the lid, and shook out the note. It said:

DEAR HUGO,

NO, I HAVE NEVER BEEN TO BORA BORA OR ATLANTIC CITY BUT I HAVE BEEN TO CLEVELAND. I ATE A GOOD CHILI DOG THERE.

GUESS WHAT? I LIVE IN THE NORTH WOODS, TOO, ON THE BANKS OF RIPPLE WORM RIVER. I LIVE WITH MY GRANDMA IN A BLUE HOUSE WITH A RED ROOF. HERE IS WHAT IT LOOKS LIKE:

NO ONE LIVES AROUND US FOR MILES
AND MILES. SOMETIMES IT GETS PRETTY
LONELY.

I HAVE SOMETHING ELSE TO TELL
YOU. IT'S A SECRET, THOUGH. LAST WEEK
WHEN I WAS IN THE WOODS, I CLOSED
MY EYES AND MADE A WISH. I WISHED
THAT I WOULD SEE A BIGFOOT. WHEN I
OPENED MY EYES, THERE HE WAS! HE
WAS HUGE AND COVERED WITH HAIR! HE
LOOKED LIKE THIS:

DO YOU BELIEVE ME? I HOPE SO,
BECAUSE IT'S 100% TRUE.

BOONE

P.S. I'M REALLY GLAD WE'RE FRIENDS,
HUGO.

So Boone was the Human Hugo had seen by the hemlock tree! Hugo looked at the drawing of the Sasquatch covered in twigs and leaves. That was a drawing of *him*!

He thought of Boone's funny sticking-

75

up hair and his eyes that looked like a Sasquatch's eyes. There was nothing scary about Boone. There was nothing bad about Boone. Gigi might be right most of the time, but this time she was wrong, 100 percent wrong.

Hugo wrote back straightaway:

DEAR BOONE,

I DO BELIEVE YOU, BECAUSE THE BIGFOOT THAT YOU SAW IN THE WOODS WAS ME!

HUGO

P.S. WE ARE CALLED SASQUATCHES, NOT BIGFOOT.

## 14

## The Last Letter

After school, Hugo didn't even stop at the Everything-You-Need General Store and Bakery. Instead he ran straight home. He flung open his bedroom door and immediately did a whoop of joy. Bobbing on the stream, caught up in a tangle of soggy leaves, was his little boat.

He opened the jar inside the boat and shook out the note. This is what it said:

DEAR HUGO,

I THOUGHT YOU WERE MY FRIEND, BUT I WAS WRONG. FRIENDS DON'T MAKE FUN OF EACH OTHER. I'M NOT DUMB. I KNOW YOU'RE NOT BIGFOOT. BIGFOOT DOESN'T WRITE LETTERS TO PEOPLE.

BOONE

P.S. THIS IS THE LAST TIME I WILL WRITE TO YOU.

Hugo felt sick to his stomach. He slumped down on his bed and read the note again. Not only had he lost his friend, but now Boone thought he was a liar. The Big Wide World had never felt so far away.

## 15

## Frog Moon Festival

The Frog Moon Festival begins at the time of day called dimmery, which is just after supper, when people like you and me begin to wonder if there is something good on TV. First, Ms. Winterbottom went outside the cave to do some Sneaking. This was to make sure no Humans were around, and there weren't.

After that came the Thwacking of the Log. Mr. Villabaloo, who was one of the tallest and strongest Sasquatches in Widdershins Cavern, found a big log. He lifted it up with a mighty effort, then thwacked the log against the trunk of a great oak tree. *BOOOOM!* It made a noise like a clap of thunder. He thwacked the tree again. *BOOOOM!* And again. *BOOOOOM!*

The sound of thunder rolled through the North Woods. Humans who lived nearby heard it and said to their families, "Sounds like a real gullywhomper of a storm is heading our way." Then they quickly shut all their windows, made sure their cat was inside, and tucked themselves in for a cozy evening at home.

After the Thwacking of the Log, all the

Sasquatches piled out of Widdershins Cavern and the festivities began. There were relay races and log-throwing competitions and a somersault area. Sasquatches are terrible at somersaults, but they love to do them, they just do.

All sorts of delicious food was laid out on a long table—sweet walnut rumples and huckleberry trifles and rosehip crunchers. And so many pies! Blueberry and gooseberry and golden cloudberry pie, and buffaloberry pie, all made from last summer's berries that had been canned especially

for the Frog Moon Festival. And at either
end of the table were jugs of sweetened
pine needle tea.

Some of the squidges wore their masks
and some didn't, but they were all laughing and screeching and running and having a great time. All ex-
cept Hugo. He sat on
an old tree stump
with his chin in his
hand, feeling rotten
about what had hap-
pened with Boone.

Suddenly a monster ran up to him and stuck its face into Hugo's.

*"Grahhhh! RAAAAAA!"* the monster said.

"Hi, Malcolm," Hugo said glumly.

"How did you know it was me?" Malcolm asked from behind his mask.

"You have acorn butter stuck to your chest hair."

"Oh." He turned to lunge at a small squidge named Pandora. *"GRAAAAAH!"* he growled very ferociously.

Pandora began shrieking.

"It's just Malcolm," Hugo told Pandora.

But Pandora kept shrieking.

"Tell her it's just you, Malcolm," Hugo said.

"Don't boss me, Captain Flapdoodle," Malcolm replied.

*"Captain Flapdoodle?"* asked Hugo, squinching up his face. "What does that even *mean*?"

Pandora's screeching grew so loud that Hugo finally stood up and whipped the mask right off Malcolm's head.

"Hey! What did you do that for?!" Malcolm said angrily.

"She needs to see that it's you under there or she won't believe it," Hugo told Malcolm.

Then two good things happened:

1. Pandora stopped shrieking.
2. Hugo had an idea.

## 16

## Ripple Worm River

There was so much going on at the Frog Moon Festival that no one noticed one little Sasquatch wandering off by himself. Hugo had decided that Boone needed to see him in order to believe that he was really a Sasquatch, just like Pandora had needed to see Malcolm to believe that he wasn't a monster.

Hugo snuck past the hemlock trees and down a hill. He walked until the trees turned into a meadow, and at the end of the meadow was Ripple Worm River. Hugo gasped when he saw it. It was a beautiful, tumbling river, all twisty and turnish. And somewhere along the banks of that river, in a little blue house with a red roof, lived Boone.

Hugo began to walk along the riverbank. Before each bend in the river, he told himself that the little blue house was certainly just beyond it. But when he turned the bend, there was only more river and no blue house. Hugo walked until his feet grew achy. Finally he had to sit down on the bank to rest his tired legs.

Maybe Boone lived very far downriver,

Hugo considered. Too far for a little Sasquatch to walk in one day.

*But when will I ever have another chance to find him?* thought Hugo. That brought him to his feet again. But the next bend in the river came, and there was still no sign of Boone's house. Then Hugo stubbed his toe painfully on a fat log that had been hidden by tall grass.

*"OWWW!"* he cried, hopping around on one foot. "Stupid log!" And he picked it up and heaved it right into the river. He watched as it hit the water with a great splash. The log then bobbed very matter-of-factly, as if it had *meant* to spend some time in the river and was glad that someone had finally flung it in. It drifted downriver in such a slow, easy way that Hugo was struck with another idea.

He rushed alongside the bank until he caught up with the log. He hesitated, looking nervously at the wide river that never stopped moving. But then he thought about Boone, and he knew he had to act quickly. With a great leap, he jumped off the bank—Sasquatches can leap like mountain goats when they want to—and he plunged into the river. He landed right beside the log, which was exactly where he was aiming to land, since Hugo couldn't swim. He wrapped his arms around the log, and off he floated down Ripple Worm River, the whole time keeping a lookout for the blue house with the red roof.

## 17

## A Wild Ride

*T*his is much better than walking, Hugo thought, as the cool river swept him along. His tired legs felt so funny and light in the water. He watched the marvelous Big Wide World as it slipped by—the blue sky above growing more purple with the dimmering. The grassy banks with the thick forest behind them.

"This must be what it feels like to sail in a boat!" he said. That made him think of sharks, and he curled up his toes nervously. But then he remembered what Gigi had said about hair balls, so it was all right again.

Though he kept his eyes on the shore, he didn't see the blue house with the red roof. In fact, he didn't see any houses at all.

Up ahead, the river was growing narrower, and there were humps of rocks along the banks. The water was moving

faster now. The log was picking up speed, bouncing and bucking wildly. If you've ever ridden on a bull, you'll understand how that feels.

Hugo struggled mightily to hold on to the log. The water kicked up and slapped his face. There was a loud *THUMP-BUMP* as his log smashed against the rocks, and Hugo was tossed off and flung into the wild, foaming water. Frantic, he flapped his arms and kicked his legs and struggled to stay afloat, but the current spun him this way and that way until finally—horribly— he was pulled beneath the water. With his head underwater, Hugo was tossed around like a sock in a washing machine. He wasn't sure if he was upside down or right side up.

Just then Hugo spotted something in the water. It was long and thin and bright yellow. He didn't know what it was, but it seemed like a good idea to grab on to it. So that is what he did. Once he grabbed it, he felt the yellow thing begin to pull him up, and in a moment his head popped out of the water, and he took the longest,

deepest breath he had ever taken in his life. The water was still thrashing around him, but he kept hold of the yellow thing, which he could now see was an umbrella. Hugo kicked his feet until, a few moments later, he had reached the riverbank and scrambled up to safety.

There, holding the other end of the umbrella, was a Human. Tall-wise, he only reached Hugo's waist, and wide-wise, he was about the same size around as one of Hugo's legs. And he had a messy tuft of hair on top of his head.

This time, though, Hugo didn't laugh at him.

"Thank you, Boone," Hugo said.

Boone's eyes were wide with astonishment.

"Holy cats," he said, "you really *are* real!"

## 18
### Boone

Boone kept staring at Hugo as Hugo collapsed on the ground and began to squeeze water out of his hair. "And you can talk!" Boone said.

"Of course I can talk," replied Hugo as he wrung himself out.

Boone leaned over and sniffed Hugo. "You don't smell like rotten eggs."

Hugo sniffed at Boone. "You don't smell like a dead porcupine," he said. He looked hard at Boone's face. "What are those dots?"

"What dots?" Boone frowned and touched his face. "Oh! You mean my freckles! I have thirty-eight of them." He pointed to one next to his right ear. "This guy is new."

"He's nice," Hugo said, because he really didn't know what you were supposed to say about a freckle.

"Lucky thing I had the umbrella with me, huh?" said Boone. "Grandma and I heard thunder a little while ago, and she made me take it with me when I went out."

Right then Hugo noticed the house behind them. It was set back in the woods, with bits of blue house and red roof peeping out through the trees.

"There's your house!" Hugo cried. "I've been looking for it."

"You have? Why?" asked Boone.

"To prove to you that I was real," said Hugo.

"Oh." Boone looked ashamed. "Yeah. I'm sorry I said all that stuff in the note."

"That's okay," said Hugo. And it really was.

"So where do you live?" asked Boone.

"In Widdershins Cavern," said Hugo. "By the five hemlock trees."

"A cave? Lucky!" said Boone. "Cryptozoolo-gists always find inter-esting things in caves, and I'm going to be a cryptozoologist when I grow up."

(This is how you say "cryptozoologist":

CRIP-TOE-ZO-OLOGIST. Practice it a few times. It's fun to say, and if you say it right, people will think you are a genius.)

"I guess there are plenty of bats and spiders in caves," said Hugo doubtfully.

"Cryptozoologists aren't looking for bats and spiders," said Boone. "They're looking for mysterious creatures. Creatures like Bigfoot."

Hugo frowned when he heard the name "Bigfoot" again. He cleared his throat.

"The thing is," said Hugo in an uncomfortable voice, "*I* don't think my feet are all that big."

"Of course they're big," said Boone. "Look." He took off his shoe and held his foot against Hugo's foot. Boone's foot was not even half the size of Hugo's.

"Well," said Hugo peevishly, "maybe it's just that *your* feet are too little."

Hugo and Boone might have gotten into an argument over this, which would have been a bad start to a new friendship. Luckily, though, Boone just grinned and said, "Hey, I can be Little Foot! That would make us Big Foot and Little Foot."

And the two of them were perfectly happy with this arrangement.

"So how do you find the mysterious creatures?" Hugo asked.

"The first thing you have to do is figure out if they're real or not," said Boone.

"How do you figure that out?"

"Well," Boone said, "the way I know they're real is that I get the shivers when I think about them."

"And *then* what do you do?" asked Hugo.

"Then you look for them. I was looking for the Ogopogo when I saw you in the water."

"What's an Ogopogo?" asked Hugo.

"It's a sea serpent. I thought I might have spotted it right before I saw you."

"Where?"

"Just up ahead." He pointed at the river, back in the direction Hugo had come from. "Want to help me look?"

Hugo nodded.

"Okay, let's go!" Boone jumped up and started running. Hugo jumped up and followed.

"Boone, guess what!" Hugo called ahead to him.

"What?" Boone called back.

"I just got the shivers!"

# 19

## The Ogopogo

A little red rowboat lay on the shore, its oars spread out on either side. Hugo thought that they looked like arms opened wide.

"Meet the *Voyager*!" said Boone, sweeping his arm toward the boat. On the back of the rowboat the word "Voyajer" was painted in white letters. "She's all mine, too."

Hugo almost said, " 'Voyager' is spelled wrong," but decided not to. Together they pushed the *Voyajer* into the river. Boone held the boat while Hugo stepped into it. Boone hopped in himself, and he pushed off with an oar.

At first Boone did the rowing. But then Hugo asked if he could try.

"Sure," said Boone, and he handed Hugo the oars. It was harder than it looked. At first Hugo could only make the *Voyajer* turn in circles. After a few minutes, though, Hugo got the hang of it. With his strong arms, he rowed the *Voyajer* along the river so fast that Boone flapped his arms in the air and laughed.

"Go, Hugo, go! We're flying!" he called out.

It *did* feel like they were flying. The

hair on Hugo's body whipped wildly in the wind. It was thrilling to be out on the water under a darkening sky. It felt like anything could happen.

"There it is, Hugo! Up ahead! The Ogopogo!" cried Boone.

Hugo stared into the distance. There was *some*thing. It looked sort of like a log, though.

In a deep voice, Boone said, "Big Foot and Little Foot raced across the water in the *Voyajer*, their triple turbo speedboat."

"What are you doing?" asked Hugo.

"Telling our story," said Boone in his regular voice.

"Why?"

"Because one day I'm going to write

books about my adventures as a cryptozo-ologist," he answered.

The dark shape in the distance disap-peared for a moment. "The Ogopogo slith-ered through the water," said Boone in his deep voice, "while Big Foot and Little Foot bravely chased it."

The dark shape reappeared now, a lit-tle farther away.

"Suddenly a storm came!" said Boone in his deep voice.

"But there isn't any storm," protested Hugo.

"I know," Boone said in his regular voice, "but it adds suspense."

"Oh," said Hugo.

"The *Voyajer* was pitching and rolling!" Boone continued in his deep voice. "The waves were as tall as a . . . as a roller coaster."

"And there were sharks," suggested Hugo, who wasn't exactly sure what a roller coaster was. "You could put that in."

"And there were loads of sharks," said Boone. "Luckily Big Foot was an expert sailor . . ."

Hugo rowed faster, his face warm with pride.

". . . and he sailed right through the storm, like a pro." Boone continued in his deep voice: "No one had ever seen the Ogopogo up close. Some said it lived in an underwater cave on a secret island."

Suddenly, up ahead, they saw a snaky hump scroll out of the water. Right after that, a head popped out of the water. It looked like a horse's head with a too-long neck. The creature twisted its neck around and looked back at them. Hugo could see the gleam of one dark eye. Then the creature dove back under the water and vanished.

For a moment Hugo and Boone were perfectly silent.

"Whoa," Hugo whispered.

"Whoa," Boone whispered back.

"It looked right at us," said Hugo.

They both stared out at the water. It was flat and still now. The Ogopogo was gone.

In his deep voice, Boone said, "'The world is full of mysteries if you just pay attention,' said Little Foot."

The sky was getting darker now. In all the excitement, Hugo had forgotten about the Frog Moon Festival. "It's getting late. I should go back home," Hugo said.

They weren't far from the five hemlocks, so Hugo began to row again.

"Steer clear of the rocks to your left," said Boone.

Hugo steered away from them.

"The river gets shallow in a minute, so bring up your oars," Boone warned. Hugo did.

Then Boone told him, "The river splits up ahead. You'll want to stay to the right!"

It turned out that Boone knew all about the Big Wide World—or at least all about

Ripple Worm River. He was an excellent Navigator. And Hugo was becoming a good sailor.

The only thing they needed was five barrels of blackberries and thirty jars of acorn butter.

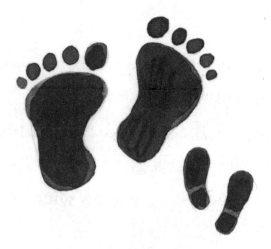

## 20

## Monsters

In no time at all they arrived at the banks of the meadow where Hugo had first set off on his journey to find Boone. Hugo and Boone dragged the boat onto the shore.

"Thank you for everything, Boone," Hugo said as he stepped out of the boat. "I'll write to you tomorrow."

"Wait," said Boone, confused. "I wanted to meet the other Sasquatches."

"Oh . . . well . . ." said Hugo uneasily. "That might not be a good idea."

"Why?" Boone's eyes grew wide. "Would they eat me?"

"Of course not!" said Hugo.

"Then why not?"

*Because the other Sasquatches will be mad at me,* thought Hugo. *Because they will say that Boone is dangerous. Because if I bring Boone back to meet them, no one will want to talk to me ever again.*

But . . . Boone had saved Hugo's life. He and Boone had chased the Ogopogo together.

They were Big Foot and Little Foot.

Hugo looked at Boone. "Are you hungry?" he asked.

"Always," said Boone.

"Well, you're about to have the best gooseberry pie in the whole North Woods. Come on."

Hugo and Boone hurried across the meadow, then up the hill and through the woods toward the five hemlocks. They could hear the sounds of the Frog Moon Festival—laughing and stomping and singing. That made them walk even faster.

Suddenly a high-pitched screech rang through the woods: *"OOOOMA! OOOOOOOOOOMA!"*

Hugo and Boone stopped short.

"What was *that*?" asked Boone.

"I don't know," said Hugo. He had never

heard anything that sounded like that—
not a bird or a bobcat or a wolf.

*"OOOOOOMA!"* The shrieking seemed
to be coming from high up in the treetops.

Hugo and Boone stared up at the hemlock trees. The light was so dim that at first
they couldn't see anything. But then Boone
pointed up at the hemlock tree farthest
from them. In a whisper, he said, "There!"

Hugo saw it, half covered by leaves. Its
gaping mouth showed two rows of pointed
teeth. Its eyes were mean yellow slits, and
there was a large spike on its head.

"What *is* that thing?" asked Boone in a
horrified voice.

Hugo knew exactly what it was. He felt
his heart begin to beat fast.

"Is it some kind of bird?" whispered Boone.

"It's not a bird," Hugo whispered. "It's a Snoot-Nosed Gint."

*"OOOOOOOMA!"* the Snoot-Nosed Gint shrieked.

The hemlock tree branches rustled wildly. Hugo could see the Snoot-Nosed

Gint's eyes staring down at him. Thinking fast, he grabbed the yellow umbrella from Boone's hands.

"Run!" he told Boone.

"What about you?" asked Boone.

"I'll be right behind you," Hugo told him.

Boone ran. Hugo turned back to the Snoot-Nosed Gint. He lifted the umbrella in one hand and pointed the tip toward the creature. With one quick step forward and a heave-ho, Hugo launched the umbrella into the air. It flew up into the tree, and a

 second later the Snoot-Nosed Gint shrieked in pain.

Hugo turned and ran as fast as a sneeze through a screen door.

## 21

### *Oooma*

Hugo crashed through the woods, running as hard as he could. Behind him he heard the terrible *KA-THUMP* of the Snoot-Nosed Gint as it leapt down from the tree. Its shrieking call of *"Ooooma! OOOOOOOOMA!"* was getting closer and closer every second.

Hugo ran through the woods and straight into the Frog Moon Festival.

But the festival was oddly quiet. The Sasquatches weren't talking or laughing or eating or somersaulting. They were all standing very still, and they were all staring at Boone, who had arrived a moment before Hugo.

"Snoot-Nosed Gint, Snoot-Nosed Gint!" Hugo screamed, warning the others.

Nobody moved. Nobody said a word.

Finally, in a quiet, scared voice, Gigi said, "That's not a Snoot-Nosed Gint, Hugo. That's a Human."

"I don't mean *him*!" Hugo said, pointing to Boone. "I mean HIM!" He turned around and pointed to the creature coming right at them. To Hugo's horror, the Snoot-Nosed Gint was as big as he was. Even more shocking, though, was that it was running on two legs. And it wasn't scaly, like a regular lizard. It was covered with thick, reddish-brown hair.

"*OOOOOMA!*" it shrieked, looking at everyone. Now Hugo could see headgear peeping out from the sides of the Snoot-Nosed Gint's head. Hugo sighed.

"Hi, Izzy," Hugo said.

"Hi, Yooho." Izzy removed his Snoot-Nosed Gint mask.

"What were you doing way up in that tree?" asked Hugo.

"Climbing. It was my Act of Bavewy," he replied. He looked at Boone. Then at Hugo.

"Yooho?" said Izzy. "Who is that oooma?" He pointed at Boone.

It was then that Hugo realized that the cry of "oooma" had only been Izzy trying to say "Human," which is very hard to say if you are wearing headgear.

"Everyone," said Hugo to all the Sasquatches, "this is my friend Boone."

"Hello," said Boone. Then he bowed to them, very deeply, which was exactly the right thing to do.

## 22

## Peepers

It took a while for Hugo to explain about Boone. He told everyone about the messages in the toy boat and about his ride on the log down the wild river and how Boone had used an umbrella to save him from drowning. While he spoke, the Sasquatches kept staring at Boone, then at Hugo, then back at Boone again. None of the squidges had ever seen a real, live Human before. Some of the grown-up Sasquatches hadn't either.

When Hugo was finished, Hugo's grandfather walked up to Boone.

"Careful!" cried Mrs. Rattlebags. "I hear they bite!"

Grandpa looked down at Boone. Boone had to tip his head way back to look up at Grandpa.

"Do you bite?" asked Grandpa.

"No," said Boone definitely. But then he added, "Well, when I was two, I bit our cat. But only because she bit me first."

Hugo's grandfather laughed. Then he shook Boone's hand—carefully, of course, since Boone's whole hand was the size of Grandpa's thumb.

"Pleasure to meet you, Boone," he said.

"No, no, no!" cried Mrs. Rattlebags. "I don't like this! He'll tell other Humans where we live. Then we'll be chased out of our lovely cave, and we'll have to live in a nasty, wet hole in a hill."

Boone stood up very straight, and with as much dignity as he could muster he said, "I promise never to tell a soul." Then he spit in his hand and crossed his heart.

"That's good enough for me," said Hugo's dad.

And slowly, Sasquatch by Sasquatch, everyone agreed. Except maybe for Mrs. Rattlebags, but that's just the way she was.

After that, the Festival continued with the Acts of Bravery. Gigi stuck her uncle's

pet rat on her head, and even though she looked like she was about to throw up, she kept him on there for a solid three minutes.

Pip sang a song, badly but loudly. Malcolm started to put a large spider in his mouth, but Mrs. Nukluk stopped him in time.

"We are performing Acts of *Bravery*, Malcolm, not Acts of *Stupidity*," Mrs. Nukluk said.

In the end, Malcolm walked across a narrow plank of wood that was balanced on two boulders, but he looked very disappointed the whole way across.

When everyone had done their Act of

Bravery, Pip said, "What about Hugo? He hasn't done his."

"Oh . . . I . . ." Hugo stammered. With everything that had happened lately, he had forgotten to choose an Act of Bravery.

"But he *did* do an Act of Bravery," said Boone. "He chucked my umbrella at the Snoot-Nosed Gint."

"It hit my wump," said Izzy, rubbing at his backside.

"But he chucked it at *Izzy*, not a Snoot-Nosed Gint," objected Pip.

"Well, he *thought* it was a Snoot-Nosed Gint," Boone argued. "That should count."

"It does count," Mrs. Nukluk declared, and no one disagreed.

*"Shhh!"* said Gigi suddenly. She tapped her ear. "Listen."

Everyone grew quiet. At first all they heard was the soft rustling of the trees in the night. But then . . . *Peep-peep! Peep-peep! Peep-peep-peeeeeep!*

"Peepers!" cried Pandora.

"*Spring* peepers," Gigi said.

For a while they all breathed in the brand-new spring air while they listened to the frogs making their *peeping* song. They listened quietly like this until someone's stomach growled very loudly. For Sasquatches, stomach growling works the way yawns do for humans. It's very catchy. Pretty soon there were so many stomachs growling that no one could hear the peepers anymore, so it was clear that it was time to sit at the table and eat.

Hugo scooped up a slice of gooseberry

pie and put it on Boone's plate. Then he put one on his own.

Boone took a bite of pie while he looked down the table at all the Sasquatches.

"A guy could never feel lonely here," he said, then sighed. Half of the sigh was happy, which means that the other half was sad.

Hugo looked down the table, too. There were grown Sasquatches and squidges and even the just-born Sasquatches (which are called chuddles). Everyone was eating and talking and laughing.

*Boone is right,* thought Hugo. *You can't ever feel lonely here. You could feel frustrated, and you could wish you had adventures in the Big Wide World . . . but you could never, ever feel lonely. And that was something.*

"If you come back tomorrow," Hugo said to Boone, "I'll show you how to play Five Rocks, Two Sticks."

"Really?"

"Definitely," said Hugo.

Boone cleared his throat and in a deep voice said, "After their adventures, Big Foot and Little Foot sat under the starry sky, eating the best gooseberry pie in the whole North Woods and making plans for tomorrow. And that's the story of how Big Foot and Little Foot became friends."

He smiled at Hugo. "The End."

Hugo smiled back.

"To be continued," Hugo said.

**ELLEN POTTER** is the award-winning author of many books for children, including the Olivia Kidney series, *Slob*, *The Kneebone Boy*, and most recently, the Piper Green and the Fairy Tree series. She lives in Maine.

**FELICITA SALA** is the self-taught illustrator of many books for children. She lives with her husband and daughter in Rome, Italy.

# ACKNOWLEDGMENTS

Sasquatches know that we all need help if we want to do things right, and that's why I want to thank my wonderful "Sasquatch Community." I was lucky enough to have Susan Van Metre as my editor. Thank you, Susan, for your sharp eye, spot-on suggestions, and especially for your kindness. I am forever grateful to my agent, Alice Tasman, who is even better than thirty jars of acorn butter. Thanks to Felicita Sala for bringing Hugo and his friends to life with her beautiful illustrations. I'm grateful for the wisdom of my superstar friends and fellow writers, Anne Mazer and Megan Shull. And finally, as always, thanks to my practically perfect husband, Adam, and my own squidge, Ian.